ALSO BY REBECKA VIGUS

Macy McVannel Novels

Cold Case: Sleeping Dogs Lie
Crossing the Line
Sanctuary

Other Novels

Out of the Flames
Secrets
Target of Vengeance

Short Stories

Broken Chains

Non-Fiction

So You Think You Want to Be a Mommy?

Poetry

Only a Start and Beyond

REBECKA VIGUS

ESCAPE

A SANCTUARY SHORT STORY

FEATURING MACY McVANNEL

Lilac
Publishing

Book cover, interior book design, and eBook design
by Blue Harvest Creative
www.blueharvestcreative.com

Published by
Lilac Publishing

ISBN-13: 978-0989098151
ISBN-10: 098909815X

Visit the author at:
www.ramblingsbyrebecka.blogspot.com
www.facebook.com/RebeckaVigusAuthor
www.twitter.com @DuchessoOfLilac

Purchase other books by Rebecka Vigus in print, eBook, or audio by scanning the QR code.

This book is dedicated to
Savannah Wise and Caitlin Turner

CHAPTER ONE

"Montgomery Law Office, how may I help you?" Maureen said reaching for a note pad.

"Maureen, it's Macy McVannel. I need to speak with Dani if she's in."

"I believe she is, let me check," placing Macy on hold, Maureen buzzes Dani's office.

"Yes?" Dani said picking up the phone.

"Detective McVannel on line one for you," Maureen tells her.

"Thank, Maureen," Dani replies then picks up line one, "Hey, Macy, what's up?"

"I have a candidate for your services."

"You don't have any competent lawyers in Rivers Edge?" Dani chuckles.

"This one needs your other specialty," Macy whispers.

"Oh, how can I help?"

"A victim age fifteen, I am taking her to the hospital and then to a safe house. Can you come?"

Dani chews the pencil in your hand, "Same safe house as Misty?"

"Safest one I know," Macy replies.

"Give me an hour," Dani says looking at the briefs on her desk, knowing they will wait.

"Thanks, see you soon," Macy says and ends the call.

Dani hangs up the phone and calls Maureen into her office. "What do I have going on today?"

"You were working on briefs, but your calendar is empty," Maureen answers.

"Good, keep it clear. I am heading to Rivers Edge. It seems Macy has found someone who needs to be rescued."

"No problem, you go take care of this unfortunate woman. I'll maintain the office," Maureen assured her. "You might want Ella to put a sandwich together for you as you will be missing lunch."

"Thanks, I'll ask her." Dani opened her briefcase, started putting in the things she would need.

Quietly Maureen left the office. She went to the kitchen knowing Dani would forget. She and Ella had become friends over the past two months she had worked here.

Ella looked up and Maureen said, "Miss Dani is going out on a call. An abused woman. Detective McVannel just called. Can you fix her something to go?"

Muttering as always Ella answered, "Of course I can. Girl is going to get herself in over her head one of these days."

Making her way back to the office, Maureen stopped to listen to the sound of laughter. Lizzy and her kids would be leaving soon. She would miss them dropping in to tell her about some new adventure.

CHAPTER TWO

Dani was coming out of her office when Ella arrived with lunch for her. "Oh, thanks, Ella," she said taking the bag. She glanced around the office, "I'll call in as soon as I can." Then she was gone.

"Girl is going to run herself ragged," Ella muttered as she made her way back to the kitchen.

Maureen just smiled. She loved working for Dani. Ella made her feel like part of the household. This would be the job she would retire from. She entered the office and went back to work.

Before she could think Ella returned, "Maureen, would you care to join me in the kitchen for coffee and a treat?"

"I'd love to," Maureen answered. She was intrigued, usually Ella just slipped in with a dish of goodies and slipped out.

In the kitchen Ella poured two cups of coffee and brought them to the table. An assortment of goodies made by Lizzy and Ella were sitting in the center. Maureen took a seat and waited for Ella.

Ella took a deep breath and began, "I hate to be a bother, but I was wondering if Miss Dani had heard anything from Misty."

"I don't think so," Maureen assured her. She reached for a cookie and continued, "Miss Dani wouldn't keep something like a letter from Misty to herself."

Ella nodded and sipped her coffee, "It's been a month and I was hoping to hear something. The holidays will be here before you know it and she will be alone."

Maureen put down her cup and reached for Ella's hand, "I know you worry, but she needs time to settle in. She will contact us when she is ready and you will be so proud of her."

"You are good to say so," Ella responded. Take as much time as you like to finish your break, I can listen for the phone." She stood and made her way to the laundry room.

Maureen finished her coffee and put the cup in the sink. She snatched a date cookie and headed back to the office. At least as far as she knew Misty had not made contact. She made a mental note to ask Dani when she returned.

CHAPTER THREE

Dani ate her lunch as she made her way to Ida Appleton's farm in Rivers Edge. This must be serious if Macy already had the victim in protective custody. *I wonder how badly beaten this one will be. Will she be ready to file for divorce and flee? Does she have children? So far, Dani had helped two women escape. Lizzy and the kids would be going soon. Her sanctuary was available at the moment.*

Finishing a bottle of water as she turned into Ida's driveway, she spotted Macy's private car. This had to be serious. She was probably bringing this newest victim home with her. Time would tell.

Macy was waiting at the door when Dani got to it. "Hey, you were quick."

"I believed you have someone in danger," Dani replied.

"Come on in, we'll fill you in." Macy held the door so Dani could enter.

Ida and a young girl were waiting in the kitchen. She hugged Dani. "I'm so glad you can help."

"Thanks, Ida, I will do the best I can," Dani said with a chuckle as she extricated herself and prepared to meet the young girl in the room. She held out her hand saying, "Hi, I'm Dani Montgomery."

The girl who took her hand whispered, "I'm Grace Dutton." Her dark hair hung to her shoulders and her brown eyes held a deep sadness.

"I put water and iced tea out for you, but I'm going to get things ready for my quilting bee," Ida told them and left the room.

Macy shrugged, "She prefers not to hear the details. I feel we are lucky she offers her home as a temporary safe haven." She pulled out a chair and indicated the others should, too. When they were seated she said, "Grace, you need to tell Dani everything you told me. She is an attorney and will know the best way to help you."

Grace took a deep breath and began, "My father has molested me since I was eight years old. He recently told me, I was too old for him. I panicked because my little sister will be eight in a few months."

"How old are you, Grace?" Dani asked already taking notes.

"I just turned fifteen. He started pushing me away a year ago when I started having periods."

"Do you have more than one sister?" Dani's mind was running at full speed.

"Two brothers in between us."

"Where is your mom?" this made a huge difference in what Dani could do.

"She died when my sister, Lucy was born. I have taken care of the younger kids."

"Has your father ever hit you?"

"Only a couple of times and not where anyone would have noticed. I need help getting my sister and me away. Joey is thirteen and Billy is eleven. Lucy was unexpected. As far as I know he's never knocked them around, but I tried my best to cover for anything they did wrong," Grace's voice waivered.

Dani suspected she had taken more abuse than she was letting on. She looked at Macy, "What kind of evidence do you have?"

"Grace had a rape kit done. It shows repeated rapes. X-rays show some broken bones, explained in medical reports as accidents. I have learned he took Grace out of town for medical care. I am having her sister removed from school and brought here. Can the girls take sanctuary with you?"

"I have an open place for them. I need to file some forms so they won't be found," Dani answered. "I would like to see if we can do something for the boys. I don't feel they will be safe left with their father."

Macy took out her phone and made a call. When she hung up she told them, "The boys will be picked up, but do you have room for them?"

"As long as the kids don't mind doubling up," Dani said. "Long term placement for four children will take some time. There is school to consider."

Grace spoke up, "We all get good grades, so taking a break should not hurt us. Can we all be together?"

"For now, yes," Dani answered. "I might be able to arrange tutoring or on-line classes so you don't get behind. The hardest thing will be not being able to go outside."

"We can do anything," Grace assured her, "I want us to be safe, but I didn't think the boys would be in danger."

"They might not be, but we are not taking chances," Macy replied. "Keeping you all safe is our primary concern.

A car pulled into the driveway, Macy sent Grace into the living room. Then she looked out the window to see Tom getting out of his family car with three children. She called to Grace, "You can come back it's your brothers and sister."

The younger children started asking questions the minute they saw Grace.

"Why did we get picked up in a police car?" Billy wanted to know.

"What is going on?" Joey asked.

"Grace, I'm scared," Lucy whispered.

Tom took charge. "Hey, kids all of your questions are going to be answered. We are going to keep you safe."

"Did something happen to Dad," Joey asked.

"No, he's fine," Tom replied.

CHAPTER FOUR

Dani made her way into Ida's living room. She pulled out her phone and called her office.

"Montgomery Law Office, how may I help you?" Maureen's chipper voice came over the phone.

"Maureen, it's Dani and I need you to listen carefully. I will be having four children arriving for sanctuary soon. Can you and Ella make sure the room is ready? Also I need Ella to somehow find a way to deliver them breakfast and dinner. I'll leave that up to her."

"I'm on it. Is there anything else you need?" Maureen asked.

"Not at the moment. I have to call Brad and see if he can meet us at the boat landing."

"Good luck," Maureen said as she hung up.

The next call Dani placed was to Brad's cell, "Stevens."

"Hey there," Dani said hearing his voice. "I need a favor."

She heard him sigh, "What do you need?"

"I need you to meet Tom Maxwell at the boat launch. Eli will also be there. There are four kids needing sanctuary and they have to come in by boat."

"How soon?"

"You tell me," she replied.

"I'm on my way."

"Thank you," she was smiling as they ended the call.

She walked in and told Macy to have Eli meet them at the boat landing. "Brad is on his way. I will feel better if Eli is with him."

"I've already called."

Dani grinned. Now came the part about getting the kids back into Tom's car and heading out.

Macy and Dani decided the girls would ride with them in Dani's car. The boys were going to ride with Tom. He was going to try to explain to the boys while not being explicit why they were being taken away.

The two car caravan started toward Willow Bend, with Dani and Macy in the lead car. Lucy sat huddled next to Grace neither saying much of anything.

In the other car, Tom tried to explain to the boys without going into detail why they were not going home. "Your dad has been doing some bad things to Grace."

Joey jumped in, "We know. She cries at night and she used to tell him to stop because he was hurting her. Is he going to hurt Lucy, too?"

"Not if we can help it," Tom answered. "We are taking you some place where you will all be safe."

"Good," Joey said. "I don't know what Dad did to Grace, I just want him to stop hurting her. I tried to talk to him about it once and he beat me. Grace told me never to talk to him about it again. He was really mean to Grace after it happened. Sometimes he made her scream."

Billy asked, "Why is Daddy a bad man?"

"I don't have the answer for you yet," Tom assured him. "I can tell you I'm working on it. Do you guys like boats?"

"They're okay," Joey answered.

Billy smiled saying, "I love them."

"Well, the good guys are escaping in a boat today," Tom said. "The good news is you will have two police officers and a pilot with super powers helping you."

"Are the girls coming, too?" Joey asked.

"Yes, they are."

"Then I'm okay with it."

The rest of the drive was quiet as the boys pondered their boat ride. It didn't take long to get to the Marina.

"Stay in the van, boys," Tom told them. "I have to meet with the skipper and the other police officer. When the girls get here, we'll go." He closed the door and locked the van.

Eli pulled up and parked beside the van. Tom motioned to the pier where Brad was gassing up the boat and getting ready. They turned to see Dani's car pull in. She and Macy got out with the girls.

Tom unlocked the van so the boys could join their sisters. With the adults crowding around them they made their way to Brad and his boat. Brad helped Grace and Lucy get in. He had them sit in the bottom of the boat. Then Eli got in. He turned to help Joey and Billy in and had them sit in the bottom of the boat. Finally with the help of all the adults a large tarp covered the children and was fastened down. Eli cast off and Brad lowered the motor into the water. As soon as they cleared the pier, Brad eased the motor on and took them into the deep river water.

"I'm going to snag a ride back with Tom," Macy told Dani. "Let me know what you need."

"Let me get the kids settled and I'll call you to get a complete briefing," Dani answered. "Then I'll start paperwork."

"We arranged to have Mr. Dutton picked up at work," Tom told her, "We are holding him on child abuse charges. He'll be arraigned in the morning."

"See if Sarah can hold the arraignment until at least ten," Dani said. "I need to have all my ducks in a row. Including a discussion with Grace about other family who might take them in."

"We'll try," Macy assured her. "The kids have clothes in a suitcase in your back seat. Now get yourself home."

CHAPTER FIVE

On her way back to the house, Dani called her office.
"Montgomery Law Office, how may I help you?" Maureen asked.

"It's Dani. Are we ready for four young visitors?"

"I think so, Ella replenished everything when Misty left," Maureen answered. "We made sure the beds are all made and the sheets and linens are clean. What else would you like?"

"I don't know," Dani said honestly. "This was not a contingent I'd planned. I just know the kids are not safe at home."

"Ella is making extra lunch today so the kids will get a hot meal," Maureen told her. "I'm not sure how it will be delivered, but it will be there for them."

"Okay, I'm also going to need to find a way to get them some outdoor time," Dani pondered. "It will be an adventure. I should be there in ten minutes and Brad and Eli are coming up river. Macy won't be far behind me."

"I'll tell Ella to expect extras for lunch and see you when you get here."

Dani hung up the phone wondering what on earth she had gotten herself into this time. The drive home took no time. Dani dropped her briefcase in her office and headed upstairs to the secret passage into the hidden chamber. She passed through the chamber and headed out the tunnel door to be on the dock when the boat arrived. As she stepped outside, she heard the boat down river. She hoped Lizzy's kids would not come running when they heard it. Dani paced as she waited for the boat to arrive. When she saw it she was surprised to see the tarp still covering the children. She prepared to help them dock.

Eli helped her tie off one end while Brad got the other. Then they carefully lifted the tarp and helped the children onto the dock. It took the kids a few minutes to orient themselves.

"Let's get you inside," Dani said leading them toward the cave door."

"What is this place?" Joey asked.

Brad answered, "This is a place where you will be safe, until we can arrange something better."

Billy looked around then asked, "Are there any pirates here?"

Smiling, Dani said, "Not for years."

Once inside with the tunnel door locked, Dani began helping the children get settled. "There are games, books, a TV and DVD player. My housekeeper will come from this direction," she pointed toward the stairs, "once a day to make sure you get a hot meal." Turning to Grace she asked, "Can you cook?"

"A little," Grace replied.

"In this cupboard are soups, the fridge holds jams, jellies, eggs, and milk. You will also find bread and peanut butter as well as lunch meat. It should be enough to feed you for a while. You will not be able to go outside for a while. I have to work on how to get you outside safely. The bathroom is stocked," Dani told her. "I will be down to check on you every day. We'll see about getting you a computer for on-line schooling so no one gets behind."

Grace shook her head as if trying to take everything in. "What will we do for clothes?"

Dani walked to the closet, "The suitcase you packed earlier, is here. I'll be sure your things get washed. If you need something not here let me know when I come down next and I'll find a way to get it for you."

"Thank you," Grace answered.

"The daybed has a pull out bed under it so you can each have your own bed," Dani said. "I'll leave it to you as to who sleeps where. We'll let you get settled, I'll be back before bedtime."

Dani, Brad, and Eli left going up into the house and exiting through the linen closet.

Ella was just coming up the stairs with a tray of food. "I'm glad you are here. Miss Macy just arrived. Those poor children." She continued on into the closet and down to feed the children lunch.

CHAPTER SIX

The children just stood looking around for a minute when every-one left. Finally Billy broke the silence saying, "This is going to be some kind of awesome adventure! I'm taking the top bunk."

Grace responded saying, "Lucy and I will take the day bed. Look guys I'm really sorry I got us into this."

"Something needed to change," Joey assured her. "We didn't like hearing you cry at night and we tried to stay out of trouble so Dad wouldn't hurt you."

"You knew?" Grace was stunned.

"We knew he was hurting you, but we didn't know how to stop it," he said frowning.

"It's going to be okay now," Grace assured him. "I don't know how long we will be here or where we will live after we leave, but we'll be together."

They heard someone coming from the house and turned to see who was coming. An elderly woman came carrying a huge tray.

"Hi, kids, my name is Ella. I'm the cook and housekeeper for Miss Dani," Ella explained as she put the tray on the table. "I made sandwiches, a salad, and there are some treats for you. I'll be down in the morning to get the tray. Any leftovers you can put in your refrigerator."

"Thank you," Grace said. "I'm Grace. This is Joey, Billy, and Lucy. We're glad you are helping to put us up. I can cook but I'm not great at it."

"Then I'll be down in a couple hours to get the tray and I'll bring you dinner tonight," Ella assured her. "You will be fine." She turned to make her way back into the house, wiping at her eyes to think one or more of these children had been abused.

Grace found paper plates for the sandwiches and bowls to put the salads in. In the fridge, she found several kinds of salad dressing and pulled out the two most likely to be used. She also found a pop for each of them. They sat down to eat.

"Who is saying grace?" she asked.

Joey piped up saying, "I'll do it." Everyone bowed their heads and Joey began, "Thank you, Father, for providing us a safe place, and people to care for us. Bless us this food we are about to eat. Amen."

Grace helped Lucy get her salad and sandwich. She made them wait to have a cookie and brownies. She could see there would be plenty left over for tomorrow. There were tuna, egg salad, and ground bologna sandwiches. The boys each ate two.

After they finished the boys started playing a video game, Lucy got onto the daybed, and Grace washed the dishes and put them away. When she turned around she found Lucy sound asleep. *Well, the day turned out to be strange and confusing for all of them.* She looked at the books on the shelf, picked one and curled up on the daybed near Lucy and began reading.

Ella found them doing those things when she came down a couple hours later. She picked up the tray quietly and told them she would be back at dinner time.

CHAPTER SEVEN

Upstairs Dani, Brad, and Eli joined Macy heading into the dining room. Lizzy and the kids were already seated. Salad, dressings, and sandwiches were on the table.

"Miss Dani," Amy said, "you didn't tell us we were having a party. Mom would have fixed something special."

Smiling Dani said, "I didn't know it was going to be."

Everyone seated themselves, Teddy said grace, and salad was passed around. Both kids started chattering while the adults at the table indulged them. When Lizzy began to stop them, Dani shook her head no. Lizzy smiled realizing something serious was going on and the children provided a welcome distraction to the others.

When lunch was over, Dani, Macy, Brad, and Eli retreated to her office. As they settled around her conference table, Dani began, "I need to know everything there is to know about this situation. I'm going to represent Grace. We also need a viable place for the children to be placed. Separating them to the foster care system would be wrong. I need to get Grace into the house again to get some belongings for the other children."

Macy said, "I can arrange to get Grace in once we have her father behind bars."

"What do you need from me?" Brad asked.

Smiling Dani responded, "Just your undying support of this program and your willingness to drop everything at a moment's notice."

Brad reached for her hand across the table and gave it a squeeze saying, "You've got it."

Eli broke the spell saying, "I'll see where the kids can be placed. It may take some time."

"I don't want them getting behind in school," Dani said. "I also need to somehow find them outdoor time."

"Let me work on it," Brad suggested. "We've almost got Lizzy's place ready for them to move in. The restaurant is not ready yet, but the living quarters are close."

"Sarah Stephens will prosecute Mr. Dutton," Macy said. "Does Grace need an attorney?"

"She might need one in order to become emancipated," Dani answered. "I just want someone looking out for her. We also need to know if there is a family member who might take them in."

"As far as we know, the mother was an orphan," Eli told her. "I'm still looking to see if she had siblings and if Mr. Dutton has family, although I'm not sure placing them with Duttons would be a good idea since Grace's testimony will put her father in jail."

"Tom said something about the boys knowing something was going on, but were helpless to stop it," Macy said. "They might be called to testify, too."

"I think family will be out of the question," Eli said. "However I'll get to work on it as soon as I get back to the office."

Brad looked at the solemn faces around the table. "I will make getting the living quarters at Lizzy's restaurant done as quickly as possible."

"Great," Dani replied, "I think we are all on the same page, the kids are our first priority."

Having set their priorities, the group broke up. Eli and Macy left of Rivers Edge. Brad stayed long enough to give Dani a breath taking kiss. "I'm so proud of what you do."

Dani went to her office to go over everything she knew about the abuse of Grace Dutton. She was glad the young girl bravely came forward. Now it was time for the adults to make sure she and her siblings were given the best chance for a new start. Running her hand through her hair, Dani sighed.

CHAPTER EIGHT

Grace could see the boys getting restless. Video games would only hold their attention so long. Lucy was starting to wake up. She was going to have to talk to them soon. She was just not sure what to say.

Billy piped up saying, "Gracie, I'm bored."

"I know and it's going to be hard to stay here," she told him. "It's the only way I knew to keep us safe. I wish I'd said something sooner."

"Well, I wish I was bigger so I could have beat Dad up," Joey said with more bravado than anything else.

"No, you don't want to beat up Dad," Grace assured him. "You want to protect Lucy from what happened to me. You wanted to make sure he didn't hit you or Billy. Most of all, you wanted to find a way to protect me. I love you for it, but it's something I had to do."

Billy shrugged his shoulder, "Either way, this is boring."

They all laughed as Lucy came fully awake. "What's so funny," she asked wiping the sleep out of her eyes.

"Being bored and not being able to do all the things we did before today," Joey answered. "But we're tough, we'll get through it."

"You're right, we'll get through this because we are together," Grace agreed. "We'll stay together when it's over."

"I'm hungry," Lucy announced.

"We have leftovers from lunch," Grace replied.

A female voice from the stairwell said, "Leftovers won't be necessary." In moments Ella appeared carrying a large covered tray. "I brought you dinner. You eat up and I'll be down later to get the tray." She turned and headed back where she had come from.

The kids gathered around the table and Grace removed the cover from the tray, setting it in the sink. Turning back she saw the eager faces of her siblings. "I think we need to say grace first."

Billy shouted, "My turn so, get over here, Gracie."

Grace joined them at the table.

"Our father, thank you for the people taking care of us and for keeping us together. Thank you for this food we are about to eat. Amen."

They helped themselves to the meal chattering and laughing the whole time. Afterward the boys asked if they could do the cleanup. Grace supervised from a distance so nothing was broken. Then they curled up on the sofa bed to watch some TV, before Grace sent them in to wash up and brush their teeth before bed.

Ella found them sitting together on the sofa bed watching TV. Her heart broke to see them looking frightened. She slipped out without saying anything.

Not long after Ella left, Grace sent Joey in to get washed up, brush his teeth, and get ready for bed. Billy followed. Then Grace got Lucy taken care of and did the same for herself.

She tucked the boys in, turning off the TV. Then she bundled Lucy in next to her. It was nice. The soft light from the hallway lulled them to sleep.

UPSTAIRS, ELLA MADE her way to Dani's office. Dinner was long over and she knew Dani would still be working for the children hidden below. She hesitated at the door.

Dani looked up sensing someone was there. "Ella, do you need something?

"Those poor children, Miss Dani," she started. "We can't keep them locked up down there for long. It's not right."

"Ella, we are working on it as fast as we can," Dani assured her. "They are children they belong in the light not hidden. Until their father is behind bars, they must be hidden. I don't like it either."

"I just wish we could let them out after dinner," Ella said. "It breaks my heart to see them like this."

"Are they complaining?" Dani asked wondering how she could make things better.

"No, they were curled up together on the daybed watching TV. I heard the oldest girl sending the younger ones into wash up and brush their teeth before bed. They don't have any idea the time."

"There are clocks," Dani replied feeling some relief. "They will know by their favorite TV shows, too. Grace has good control. I am more worried about their education being neglected."

"I'm sure you will find a way," Ella said softly. She realized Dani was also concerned for the children which eased her mind. Adults in the hidden room were one thing, but children presented different problems. Right now they had Lizzy and her kids. "I'll let you get to your work."

"Good night, Ella," Dani said, "Thank you for taking this on."

Ella nodded and turned to leave.

"Wait!" Dani called out.

Returning to the office, Ella wondered what had been forgotten.

"This came today," Dani said handing Ella an envelope.

"Thank you, Miss Dani," Ella said the tears in her eyes flowed as she recognized Misty's handwriting. She clutched the letter to her chest as she turned to leave the office.

Dani found herself trying to figure out what to do for the children. Moving them from place to place was not a good idea. She hoped one of her teammates would come up with something and soon.

CHAPTER NINE

M acy showed up at Dani's early. Ella brought them coffee and coffee cake to the office. Closing the door behind her as she left.

Maureen came in to find Dani's door closed and went to the kitchen to see Ella. "Do you know who is in with Miss Dani?"

"Miss Macy came early, I took them some coffee cake for breakfast," Ella replied offering Maureen a cup of coffee and some coffee cake.

Maureen took them and sat at the table, "Is there a problem?"

"I think it has to do with our newest visitors," Ella replied.

"Okay, I can just handle the routine stuff until I get other orders," Maureen let her thoughts out. "Thanks, Ella." She picked up her coffee and coffee cake heading toward the office.

Upstairs she heard the voices of Teddy and Amy as they got themselves ready for the day. On the surface, things were normal. She went to her desk, ate breakfast, and got ready to begin her day.

Moments later, Dani stepped out of her office. "Maureen I need to go get one of our guests. Do you know if Ella took them breakfast yet?"

"I have no idea," Maureen answered.

Dani headed for the kitchen. "Ella," she said entering, then spied the tray the woman held. "I'll take it. I have to bring Grace up for court and to get things for her siblings from their home."

Ella handed Dani the tray and walked behind her as she went up the stairs. She made sure the hall was clear before she let Dani into the linen closet and the hallway it hid. She checked on Teddy and Amy who were almost dressed for breakfast.

"If you two are quick, I know there will be a treat for you for breakfast."

The children picked up speed and then went to the kitchen with Ella. They found their mother already there. On the table were fresh baked blueberry muffins. Laughing and giggling they joined their mom at the kitchen table.

IN THE HIDDEN room, Maureen found the children up and dressed. She set the tray on the table and took the lid off. There were blueberry muffins and oatmeal. Butter, milk, and orange juice came out of the small fridge and landed on the table.

Maureen motioned Grace aside, "Can I get you to bring your breakfast with you?"

"Sure, where am I going?"

"To Miss Dani's office. Detective McVannel is there and she will be taking you to court and to your home afterward to get more things for you and your siblings."

Grace hesitated, turned to the other children and said, "I need you to be on your best behavior for a few hours. I have to go to court and then I'll be stopping to get some things from our house. Do the dishes when you are done and then find something to play with."

The kids looked at her and nodded in the affirmative. Lucy tugged at her hand, "Can you bring my blanket and my baby doll?"

"You bet I can, Lucy," she said as she hugged the little girl she was trying so hard to protect. "Remember you have to stay in this room."

She turned to Dani saying, "I'm ready." Snagging a muffin, a bowl of oatmeal and a spoon, she scooped up the milk carton and poured some into her bowl. Then she followed Dani up the stairs.

At the door to the linen closet, Dani motioned for Grace to wait, stuck her head out and saw the coast was clear. Listening she heard voices in the kitchen. She motioned to Grace to follow her and led the way to the office. If Grace was surprised by what she saw, she said nothing.

Inside the office they went to Dani's office and she closed the door. Grace went to the conference table to eat her breakfast. The two women gave her time.

Macy said, "Grace, this is how it's going to work today. We have a preliminary hearing. ADA—Assistant District Attorney-Sarah Stephens will be representing you. Dani and I will be there with you. Dani is going to make sure your interests are upheld. She's also going to ask the judge to grant her custody of you and your siblings for the time being. You will not be considered fugitives or runaways. After court, Dani and I will escort you to your house, where you can get some belongings for you, your brothers, and your sister. Then you will return here to the secret hideaway. Any questions?"

"Only one. Will we have to stay inside forever?"

Dani was quick to answer, "No, I am working on getting you into my house and able to run and play in the backyard. I am also looking into some on-line education classes. It won't be the same as being in school with your friends, but it will keep you up with your class so none of you has to repeat."

Nodding her head yes, Grace responded, "We are doing well in the hidden place, it's just not being able to run and get rid of some of the steam. Thank you for considering our schooling. We will do whatever is asked of us."

"Great! I also have a wonderful person looking for a permanent place for the four of you," Dani told her. "I have made it clear you are not to be separated."

"Oh, thank you," Grace sighed. "I can't tell you how much it means to us to stay together."

"If this is all," Macy started, "we need to get on the road. I assume you will want to ride with Dani." She directed her statement to Grace.

"Yes, please, if it's okay."

"It is."

The three of them stood, Dani grabbed her purse. They left the office, Dani stopping to tell Maureen where she would be. Then they were out the front door and on the way to Rivers Edge.

When they arrived at the courthouse, Dani showed Grace what she had to do to get through the metal detector. They waited outside the courtroom on the benches until they called Grace's name. Together they went inside. Grace made her way to the witness stand and Dani took a seat behind Sarah Stephens but where she could see Grace and Grace could see her.

Grace was sworn in.

"Please state your name for the court," Sarah told her.

"Grace Dutton."

"Grace, we understand you have been abused for years. Do you see your abuser in the courtroom today?"

"Yes."

"Can you identify him for the court?"

Grace pointed to the defendant's table saying, "My father, James Dutton."

"Thank you, Grace."

Sarah turned to the defendant's table and said, "Your witness."

Her father's lawyer stood, buttoned his suit coat, and approached Grace.

"Good morning, Miss Dutton."

"Good morning."

"You don't like your father do you?"

"I have mixed feelings," Grace replied.

"Would you explain to the court your mixed feelings?"

"He's my father so I love him, but he's done things to me which no father should do to his child."

"Aren't your accusations against your father because he wouldn't let you go to a dance?"

"No, I've never asked to go to a dance."

"How is it a fifteen year old girl has never gone to a school dance?"

"I stayed home to take care of my siblings. Besides I believed everyone knew what my father was doing to me and just didn't care."

"How would everyone know if you didn't tell them?"

Grace stammered, "I, I don't know. I just felt like they knew."

"Who is your best friend?"

"I don't have one."

"You expect us to believe you have no one you confide in and talk to about your dreams?"

"I don't know if you'll believe it or not, but I have never had a best friend. My mom died when I was eight. I've had to look after the little ones when I wasn't in school. There was no time for playing."

"Yet there was time for your father to abuse you?"

"He did it at night, when he thought the others were sleeping."

"Your medical records show you are sexually active. Are you sure it wasn't your boyfriend you had sex with?"

Grace's look could have frozen the lawyer, "I don't have a boyfriend. My father has molested me since I was eight and a half years old. I begged him to stop. I cried when he hurt me. I had trouble walking. I finally had enough and reported him."

"So, you say."

Sarah Stephens was on her feet, "Objection, your Honor, badgering the witness."

"Sustained, Mr. Becker, you need to back off this witness."

Grace took a deep breath.

"No further questions." Becker turned and walked back to his seat.

"You may step down young lady," the judge told her.

As Grace stepped down and walked toward Dani, she could feel her legs shaking.

The judge said, "At this time I see sufficient reason to hold the defendant over for trial. Bail is revoked and he will be held in custody for the safety of his daughter." He banged the gavel, then said, "Ten minute recess."

Sarah turned to Grace, "You did a great job. These are the same type of questions you will be asked during the trial."

"Okay."

Grace felt numb. She was humiliated. All she wanted to do was get home and shower.

Dani spoke next, "Grace, we are going to another court room where I am going to ask to be appointed legal guardian of you, your brothers, and your sister. Do you have any objection to this?"

"No," Grace almost shouted. "I want you to be able to take care of us and find us a real home. One where we don't have to live in fear."

"Then let's go."

Dani led Grace from the court room. Sarah followed them. She sat behind them as Dani and Grace took their places at the defendant's table.

Becker had set himself at the plaintiff's table. He looked full of himself. Dani wondered who James Dutton wanted his children to go to.

Grace whispered under the breath, "I don't like *that* man. He looks more like a crook than a lawyer."

Patting her hand, Dani said, "He's not the greatest lawyer around. He loses more often than he wins."

"Good let him lose today."

Dani smiled as the bailiff announced, "All rise for the Honorable Judge McAdams."

Everyone in the court room stood as the judge entered and took her seat. "Be seated." Everyone sat.

"I see the case before us has to do with the guardianship of four minor children. Mr. Becker, whom do you represent and what are the wishes?"

"I represent the children's father, your Honor," Becker replied. "He wishes to retain guardianship of the children."

"Why isn't he here?"

"He is currently in the county lock-up awaiting trial on another matter."

"Who does he think will take care of them while he is incarcerated?"

"He expects his eldest daughter, Grace to continue caring for he siblings and has left money with me to provide for their needs."

"Hmm, Miss Montgomery, I see you are here. What is your involvement in this case?"

"I represent the interests of the Dutton children. Their father will be tried for the sexual abuse of his daughter Grace. It has come to my attention he has beaten the boys when they have tried to defend Grace. I am petitioning the court for guardianship until the children can be placed in a permanent home."

"Are you planning to separate the children?"

"No, your Honor," Dani answered. "It is my plan to place them together in a home."

"She plans to see they are institutionalized, your Honor," Becker blurted out.

"Is this true, Miss Montgomery?" the judge asked.

"No, your Honor. The children will remain with me until they can be adopted together into a family."

"I've heard enough. I have one question for Grace. What are your feelings on this?"

"I'd like my brothers, sister, and I to be with Miss Montgomery," Grace answered. "I feel we are safe with her."

"So saying, I am awarding guardianship of the Dutton children to Miss Danielle Montgomery, until such time as a home can be found for them. Miss Montgomery, you will be expected to send a monthly report on the children to this court. We are dismissed." The gavel came down as Becker came off his chair to protest.

He looked at Dani, "I'm going to appeal this."

Smiling she responded, "Be my guest." She took Grace's hand and they walked out of the courtroom. Macy was waiting for them outside.

"I think we're going to have a problem with Mr. Becker, the lawyer for James Dutton. Can you keep him busy while Grace and I go get some things for the kids? Then we need to get out of town."

"Not a problem," Macy responded as she walked over to where Mr. Becker was coming through the front doors. "Mr. Becker, a word with you please."

Becker was anything but pleased as he watched Dani and Grace walk to the parking lot.

"Can I get you to come to my office with me?" Macy asked. "I need to go over some things about the Williams case with you."

"Williams case?" he asked as he turned to follow her to the police station. "I don't have a Williams case."

"Mr. Williams is next door screaming about you being his lawyer and how he won't do any talking until you arrive." Macy almost snickered as Mr. Williams was a drunken vagrant sleeping it off in a cell.

"Well, let's hurry this up."

Macy knew he had planned to follow Dani. She was glad someone picked Mr. Williams up for a hot meal and a place to sleep. She knew he would play along with anything they wanted.

CHAPTER TEN

Dani and Grace made their escape out of the back of the parking lot. Dani drove the three blocks to the Dutton home and accompanied Grace inside where she grabbed a couple of suitcases and headed to the bedrooms. In the boys room she picked up a couple hand held games, their IPods, and several changes of clothing and some underwear and socks.

Then she headed to Lucy's room, it was little more than a closet. She picked up her favorite blanket and her baby doll. Then she added clothes and underwear along with a couple pair of pajamas and her robe.

She wasted little time and went to her room. She grabbed a couple books she was reading for school, some sidewalk chalk although she wasn't sure where she would use it. She picked clothing, hair ties, and some nail polish. Then she added underwear and socks.

Turning to Dani she asked, "Can I pick up some of the snacks we have in the kitchen?"

"You may take anything you want," Dani assure her.

Grace picked up a couple photo albums and a framed picture of a woman who must have been her mother. Then she headed for the kitchen grabbing some granola bars, a couple boxes of cereal, and hot chocolate packages.

"You know," Dani said, "I'd be happy to buy you anything you need."

"I appreciate it, but I knew we had these items," Grace assured her. "Depending on how long we are with you, I might need you to replenish them."

"Anytime."

"Well, I can't think of anything else," Grace said looking around. Then she grabbed an afghan from the sofa.

"Let's go home, then."

Dani grabbed one of the suitcases and the bag of food. They went out to the car, loaded it, got in, and prepared for the ride to Dani's. Grace felt safe for the first time since her mother died.

On the ride home, Grace spent time hugging the afghan. Dani finally asked her about it. "Is the afghan something your mother made?"

Grace nodded yes. "I wish I could crochet."

"I think we can get you some lessons in crochet if you really want to learn."

"Oh, I do. I want to make each of the kids an afghan. Something they will have to connect them to me even if we are far apart," Grace told her. "My mom is in Heaven, but when I'm wrapped in this I know she is near."

"Well, then I guess crochet lessons are in order. Then when Lucy is old enough, you can teach her," Dani suggested.

"I'd like to," Grace told her. "I could share something with her, she could one day share with her daughter or granddaughter. Miss Dani, how do you think of these things?"

"Just part of my job," Dani assured her. "I care about the people I give sanctuary to and want to make them comfortable."

"Detective McVannel was right, you are an angel on earth."

Dani blushed and continued driving.

ONCE BACK AT Dani's she put Grace in her office until she could find clear access to the linen closet. Ella came to the rescue announcing lunch was being served. After the children and Lizzy were in the dining room, Dani and Grace made their way to the linen closet with the two suitcases and the sack of groceries.

They found the other three children waiting. Joey and Billy were playing video games and Lucy was curled up sleeping. Grace put the afghan on Lucy. Then she opened the suitcase containing the boys' belongings. Both boys eagerly took their hand held games and scooted to their bunks Grace put the rest of their things away. Then she put her own things away. She left Lucy's things in the suitcase until she woke.

Turning to Dani she said, "Thank you again for everything."

"I suspect your lunch will be down shortly," Dani said then she returned to the house.

"I like her," Billy said. "She seems real nice."

"She is," Grace told him. "What you don't know is this room is part of her house. At the top of the stairs you enter a linen closet and then you go into her house. She has her law office here, too. She will take good care of us."

"Why can't we stay in her house?" Joey asked.

"She has another family she rescued staying in her house," Grace explained. "She runs a program to rescue abused people and set them up someplace else when they are free of their abuser."

"Wow, we are lucky," Joey said. "I'm glad you finally told on Dad."

"I saw him in court today," Grace whispered.

"Did they put him in jail?" Billy wanted to know.

"Until time for the trial," Grace said.

"Will you have to testify, Gracie?" Joey was all serious now.

"I will," she answered. "They might even ask you, but I'm not sure."

Joey puffed up his chest, "I'll be ready and I'll tell the truth about him hurting you."

"Can I, too?" Billy wanted to know.

"It's up to the ADA and Dad's lawyer," Grace said. "I think Billy you might be too young, but we'll find out."

"Can I at least come?" Billy asked.

"I don't know," Grace told him, "but I'll ask."

"Cool," he responded and climbed back onto his bunk to play with his handheld game.

Ella showed up a short time later with soup, sandwiches, and cookies for them to eat. They looked much happier than they had yesterday. "Miss Grace, when I come down to pick up the dishes if you'd like to start those lessons you and Miss Dani spoke about, I'll be ready," Ella said setting the tray on the table.

"I'd like to," Grace said shyly.

Ella smiled and left the children to their lunch. She knew they would do the dishes before she came back. She would start Grace making dish cloths.

The children ate lunch, cleaned up, and did the dishes. Then Lucy laid down to take a nap. The boys retreated to their bunks to play with their video games. Grace was stacking dishes on the tray when Ella returned.

"You can leave those for now," she said pulling out a chair at the table. "I'm going to start you on the easiest thing I know. I brought enough yarn for you to practice and make several."

"What will we be making?" Grace asked.

"Dish cloths," Ella answered. She began by showing Grace how to hold the yarn and use the crochet hook. There were several starts before they got one right. When Ella took the tray upstairs, Grace was halfway through her first dish cloth. Ella was smiling.

THINGS RAN SMOOTHLY for about a week. Dani had managed to get the kids enrolled in an on-line classroom. The boys were less than thrilled, but they did what was required of them. They learned to take turns quizzing each other on spelling. The only thing Dani had not been able to supply them with was outdoor time.

Lizzy's living quarters could not be opened for her until the restaurant was ready to open. Brad had his team working overtime, but it felt like they were getting nowhere.

Dani had talked to Grace and Joey the day before. Both of them would be required to give testimony, Billy and Lucy being too young. They would both be in the courtroom with Dani. She had arranged for Sarah to call Joey first. It was going to be a big day for the four of them and probably the last time they would ever see their father again.

Grace had the kids up early. They had eaten bowls of cereal and brushed their teeth. Dani came down and they were ready for her. She could see they would be a formidable team. If push came to shove, they had each other's back.

"If you're ready, let's be off," Dani said.

They started up the stairs, at the last moment, Lucy grabbed her blanket. Dani smiled knowing it as security for those times Grace was not present.

They drove silently to Rivers Edge. Macy met them outside the courthouse. She had Dani step aside.

"Grace, take them through the metal detector and take a seat on the bench," Dani instructed.

Grace gave an affirmative nod and led her siblings inside. After they passed through the metal detector they took a seat waiting for Dani and Macy to join them.

"Eli is coming. He will be here any moment with prospective parents for the children. They will sit in the back of the court room until we are done today. They'd like to take the kids to lunch and get to know them," Macy told her.

"They are willing to take four kids? And Eli has checked them out?" Dani asked.

"He has and they come highly recommended. The woman is his niece and she is a child psychologist."

Dani let out the breath she had been holding. This could be good for the kids. "Okay, let's get inside."

She and Macy headed into the courthouse to join the children.

CHAPTER ELEVEN

Dani entered the courtroom with Billy and Lucy. She had explained to them what was going to happen and told them everyone had to remain quiet. Macy stayed with Grace and Joey until it was their turn.

Lucy quietly asked, "Where will my Daddy be?"

"He will sit at the table over there. Don't worry, Lucy, he will not be allowed to talk to any of you."

"Good," she whispered.

Dani could not imagine what was going through Lucy's head, but she would stand between the little girl and the evil who was her father. She put one child on each side of her. Lucy got so close Dani thought she had somehow attached herself physically to her side.

Mr. Becker arrived at the defense table just as Mr. Dutton was led in. Lucy gasped seeing her father in handcuffs and leg irons. She moved closer to Dani. Mr. Dutton looked right at Dani. As he sat, he spoke to his lawyer who turned to look in their direction. Billy sat ramrod straight staring at the front of the room. Dani took his hand and he squeezed it.

The bailiff said, "All rise for the Honorable Judge Harold Williams."

Everyone in the court room stood. Each of the children held one of Dani's hands. The judge seated himself saying, "Be seated." Everyone sat back down.

"Are the parties all present and ready to begin?"

"Yes, your Honor," Sarah Stephens replied.

"No, your Honor," Mr. Becker began, "my client objects to his youngest children being in the gallery."

"Miss Stephens?"

"Your Honor, the children's interests are with their guardian, Miss Dani Montgomery," Sarah replied.

"Miss Montgomery, what do you have to say?"

Dani stood saying, "Your Honor, the children have asked to be here to give moral support to their older siblings who will be giving testimony. We will be leaving the gallery and the courthouse as soon as they are finished."

Judge Williams having heard enough said, "The children are allowed to remain. Let's begin. Ms. Stephens call your first witness."

Sarah who had been standing said, "The state calls Detective Macy McVannel."

Macy entered from the hallway and walked to the witness stand where she was sworn in.

"Please state your name for the record."

"Detective Sergeant Macy McVannel."

"Detective McVannel, can you tell us how you became involved in this case?"

"Through a program at Rivers Edge High School which puts a liaison officer in the building. Grace Dutton came to me for help."

"What kind of help did she need?" Sarah asked.

"She informed me her father, James Dutton, had been abusing her."

James Dutton shouted, "It's a lie. You put *that* in her head."

Judge Williams brought down the gavel, "Silence! Mr. Becker, get your client under control or he will be removed and will watch his trial on video."

"Yes, your Honor," Becker replied pulling James into his seat and giving him whispered instructions.

Sarah returned to Macy, "Why did she come forward now?"

"She told me her father started molesting her when she was eight years old, about six months after her mother died. Her younger sister will be eight soon. She was worried he would start abusing her."

Dani felt Lucy squeeze closer to her.

"What did you do then?" Sarah asked.

"I signed Grace out of school and took her to the women's clinic. There they did a rape kit, pelvic exam, and general physical. It was determined she had been raped repeatedly for years. They did find semen which when tested showed her father's DNA. My partner and I obtained a court order to remove the other three children. We picked them up and moved them to a safe place."

"Thank you." She turned and walked to her table and sat.

Mr. Becker hauled himself out of his chair and walked toward Macy, "Have you heard other stories like this?"

"In my years as a police officer, yes."

"Since providing this liaison service, have any other children come forward to claim abuse by their parents?"

"We've investigated two or three. None to this extent."

"You're telling the court you have not investigated other cases the way you investigated this one?"

"No, I'm saying this is the worst one we've investigated. One was one parent using the child in a malicious divorce and the facts did not prove the case. In another, the father was sentenced to a year in jail, ordered to a substance abuse center on release for beating his wife and children. None have been connected to sexual abuse."

"So, you have no axe to grind with Mr. Dutton?"

"I have no axe to grind with any perpetrator who comes before me."

"Thank you."

Judge Williams said, "You may step down."

Macy left the courtroom as Sarah called, "The state's next witness is Grace Dutton."

Macy held the door for Grace, she gave the girl a hug and whispered, "You can do this." Then let the door close and she joined Joey on the bench while they waited.

Grace was seated and sworn in.

"Please state your name for the record."

"Grace Dutton."

"Grace, why did you seek out Detective McVannel?"

"My father had been abusing me since I was eight."

"Why didn't you seek help sooner?"

"I didn't know who to tell."

"You didn't have a neighbor or relative you could tell?"

"There were neighbors, but I didn't know who would believe me, who I could trust. I was just a kid."

"What made you speak up now?"

"I am afraid my father is going to start molesting my little sister. I've seen him looking at her funny."

"Why would he pay attention to her now?" Sarah asked.

"She will be eight in a few months, almost the age I was when my father started molesting me."

"To your knowledge, did your father molest your brothers?"

"As far as I know he only beat them."

"Thank you, Grace."

Mr. Becker rose as Sarah returned to the prosecution table. He walked toward Grace.

"Isn't it true you were just seeking attention?"

"No, I don't seek attention."

"Isn't it true you lied after having sex with your boyfriend?"

Grace took a deep breath, "I have no time for friends, boys or girls. I am busy with school and taking care of my brothers and sister. I don't even have a boyfriend."

"A cute girl like you, surely some boy must come by the house to see you."

"No, no one comes to see me."

"Do your brother's have friends who come to the house?"

"Yes. They play on a little league team and their teammates sometimes come to the house."

"Do these same boys spend the nights?"

"No, we don't have people spend the night."

"Where are your grandparents?"

"My mother's parents are dead. I have no idea where my father's parents are. I've never met them."

"Didn't an aunt or some other relative step in to help when your mother died?"

"People brought food for the first couple of weeks, but no one helped me with the little ones. My dad was out of it for a long time, then when he seemed to come back to us, he started to molest me."

"And you're sure he wasn't just trying to comfort you?"

"For seven and a half years? I think I would know the difference between comfort and what he was doing."

"Do you blame your father for your mother's death?"

"No, why would I? She died in a car accident."

"Was your father with her?" Becker pushed.

"No, he was at work."

Becker was hoping to see a tear when he asked, "Where was your mother?"

"She was on the way to a doctor's appointment. She was hit by a car, they were able to save Lucy, but not my mom. She had pushed Billy out of the way so he wasn't hurt."

"Isn't it true your father came to your room when he heard you crying for your mother?"

"No, he snuck into my room long after my mom was gone. He touched me where he shouldn't have. Later when I was older he took my virginity and made me do things to him. It had nothing to do with my mom."

"That's all."

"You may step down, young lady," Judge Williams told her softly.

Grace walked to the gallery and slid in so she was on one side of Lucy and Dani was on the other side. Dani squeezed her hand and Grace squeezed back.

Sarah said, "The state calls Joseph Dutton to the stand."

The door at the back of the courtroom opened and Joey walked in with Macy next to him. Macy slid in with Grace, Lucy, Dani, and Billy as Joey continued to the witness stand. After he was sworn in, Sarah said, "Please state your name for the record."

His voice clear, Joey responded, "Joseph Dutton."

"Now, Joey, I want you to take a deep breath and relax," Sarah began. "Then I want you to tell the court what you heard at night."

Joey took a deep breath, let it out, and began, "Most nights after Dad thought we were sleeping I'd hear him go into Gracie's bedroom. She'd plead with him not to hurt her again. When he ignored her, she begged him to stop. He'd hurt her and then leave and go to his room. I could hear her crying. A couple times I went to check on her, but she would send me away. I wanted to help, but Dad's bigger than me. Then if Billy or I did something to get in trouble he'd take the belt to our backsides. Gracie always came to comfort us. She told us not to make him angry."

"Did you know what your father was doing to make Grace cry?"

"Not at first, but later I figured it out. It wasn't right for him to do those things to her."

"Did he ever hit Grace or Lucy?"

"I didn't see him hit them. I think he just hit me and Billy."

"Thank you, Joey."

Sarah walked back to the table and sat while Mr. Becker approached Joey.

"Joey, why are you hear today?"

"To tell everyone, my dad is a bad man. He hurt Gracie."

"Did you ever see him hurt Grace?"

"No, I only saw her after. I remember seeing the blood and she tried to hide it."

"What blood did you see, Joey?"

"It was on her sheets and nightgown. She didn't hear me come in. I knew it was wrong. But I was just a little kid. Me and Billy were trying to make a plan, so he wouldn't hurt Gracie anymore or start hurting Lucy."

"Who told you he was going to hurt Lucy?"

"No one told me, I saw him watching her. It was creepy."

"Do you like your dad, Joey?"

"I don't like the things he does."

"But do you like him?"

"No, he's a bad man."

Becker shook his head and threw up his hands. "I'm done and I'd like this witness' testimony stricken from the record as non-responsive."

"Objection, your Honor!" Sarah was on her feet in a flash. "He told the truth as he knew it."

"Sustained. We already covered this Mr. Becker. The boy's testimony remains." He turned to Joey, "You may step down, son."

Joey stepped down and walked to where everyone was sitting. Macy stood and they all walked of quietly out the courtroom. Eli was waiting for them with a young couple.

The boys went to Eli and greeted him. Eli hugged both of them then stepped back and said, "I'd like you to meet Cara and Bryce Nichols. They would like to get to know the four of you. See they cannot have children and they think you might fit well in their home. They have a horse farm a few hours from here. If it's all right with you, they would like to take you to lunch. I suggested you might want to go across the street to Dollie's Deli. What do you say?"

"Can we, Gracie?" the boys chimed in. "Can we please?"

Grace smiled watching her brother's reactions. Then she turned to Lucy, "Well, Kiddo, what do you think, shall we go to lunch?"

Smiling, Lucy nodded her head yes.

"I guess it's settled then, we'll accept your invitation to lunch."

Cara smiled and Grace felt the warmth of her smile. She held out her hand to the older woman and they left the courthouse heading for the deli.

"Well, guys what next?" Eli asked.

"I'm going back in to see how the trial goes," Dani told him.

Macy smiled, "I could use some lunch, if there's an offer."

Grinning Eli said, "There's always an offer, I packed us a picnic. It's still warm enough."

Together they left the courthouse for lunch. Dani quietly went back in and sat in the back of the courtroom to see what kind of defense Mr. Becker was going to try to offer for James Dutton's reprehensible actions.

CHAPTER TWELVE

Across the street the children with Cara and Bryce had snagged a table and were discussing menu.

Lucy asked, "Do they have mac and cheese and could I have a hot dog, too?"

"You sure can, sweetie," Cara responded with a smile.

Lucy gave her a tentative smile and Cara's heart melted.

The boys were deciding about what to have on their cheeseburgers, when Bryce suggested, "Why don't we have them bring a plate of tomatoes, onions, lettuce and pickles. Then we'll decide when our burgers arrive?"

Billy piped up, "I like it. Can I have fries, too?"

"Sure you can," Bryce said ruffing Billy's hair.

Cara turned to Grace, "What would you like, Grace?"

Grace looked up from the menu, "I think a bacon, lettuce, tomato sandwich."

"Sounds like a winner to me," Cara said smiling. "I think I'll have one, too."

The waitress took the orders and returned a few minutes later with drinks for everyone. When she left, Grace asked, "Are you sure you want all four of us?"

"We sure do," Bryce answered. "I need boys so I'm not out-numbered when we decide what to do. And girls just make a family complete."

Cara rolled her eyes, "Grace, I have always wanted children, but am not able to have them. We have a huge house and a horse farm because we planned on a big family. The four of you would fill the emptiness in our house and make it a home.

"Does that mean you'd be my real mommy?" Lucy asked.

"It does, Miss Lucy," Cara answered. "Would that be okay with you?"

Joey had been listening. He asked, "Does it mean Gracie can do things like other kids her age? You know like dances and boyfriends?"

Bryce looked at Grace as he answered, "If that's what she wants, Joey. She can join after school clubs or tryout for sports, whatever she is interested in."

Grace blushed. She was thrilled Joey was still trying to look out for her. She asked, "When do we have to decide?"

"When it feels right," Cara answered. "We'll spend time with you. You can come visit our ranch and we'll get to know each other before we make any decision."

Lunch arrived before anyone could say anything else and they all started eating. Grace thought maybe angels were watching over them. She wanted this to work, not for herself so much, but for the younger ones.

When they finished lunch, Bryce asked, "Would anyone like to go to the park?"

A chorus of yeses were his answer. He paid the bill and they left the deli walking down the street to the city park. It didn't take long for the kids to find the playground. The boys running through the fort and Grace pushing Lucy on the swings. Bryce and Cara walked to the swings, "What if I give Lucy pushes and let Grace and Cara go talk girl talk?"

"Okay, Mr. Bryce," Lucy said.

Grace turned to Cara and the two of them took a walk along the edge of the river. "I want to be your friend, Grace. I can't be the mom you lost, but I can help you if you'll let me."

"I want this to work," Grace told her. "The younger kids need a good home to grow up in. I won't fight you, Cara."

Cara nodded. It was not the answer she hoped for, but she knew it was a start. "So, what do you want to do after high school?"

"I never thought much of it," Grace admitted. "There wasn't going to be money for me to go to college and I would have needed to take care of the little ones."

"Well, if we become a family, there will be money for you to go to college," Cara told her. "You can go away to school or do two years at the junior college and then go away. It will be up to you. Is there anything you are interested in?"

"I like art, but I don't know if I could do it for a career."

"What kind of art do you like?" Cara wanted to know.

"I love scenery," Grace sighed. "I like painting places which are beautiful. Many come out of my own mind."

"Someday I hope you'll show me some of your work."

"If I ever get it back," Grace said. "It's all in the art room at the high school. Mrs. Wellesley made me think I could really be someone."

"You already are someone, Grace," Cara assured her. "If you have talent, we need to help you nurture it so you can grow and get better. I'll see if Eli or Macy can help you get your art work back. Would you like a studio?"

"Only famous artists have studios," Grace told her.

"Not true. There is a little studio on our ranch," Cara told her. "We don't use it."

"I don't know what to say."

"Don't say anything until you see it," Cara told her. "We are hoping to take you kids to the ranch for the weekend. You can see it then."

They were back at the playground, where Bryce and Lucy had joined the boys is a siege on the fort. The laughter of the kids, stopped Grace. Then she smiled.

They joined the others for the walk back to the courthouse to meet Dani and go back to her hidden room.

CHAPTER THIRTEEN

The kids piled into Dani's car. She listened as they talked, smiling at what she heard.

"Did you know Bryce played baseball in college?" Joey wanted to know.

Billy piped in, "He said he'd help me learn to pitch."

Not to be left out, Lucy said, "He told me he would always be there to help me and would get me my own pony."

Grace answered, "I didn't know Bryce played baseball, I'm sure he'll be able to teach you to pitch, and Lucy, I know you'll love having a pony and learning to ride."

"Gracie, what did you and Cara talk about?" Lucy asked.

"We talked about being a family and how they would look out for all of us and she wants to be my friend."

"But, wouldn't she be our Momma?" Lucy wanted to know.

"Yes, she would," Grace answered. "If you want her to be and the judge says it's okay." She looked at Dani and asked, "How long will it take? I know they'd like us to spend the weekend with them."

Smiling Dani answered, "Of course you can spend the weekend with them. I think it would be wonderful to see how you all function as a family. As to how long it will take, it depends on the judge and the recommendations from Eli and me."

"Miss Dani, would you recommend it please?" Joey's earnest voice reached her from the back seat.

"Joey, let's see how the weekend goes. If you still think I should recommend them after spending the weekend, we'll talk about it. I know Eli has already done a background check," she assured him.

"Why did they need to have their background checked?" Billy asked.

"So we know it's a safe place for you and they have the resources to support four children," she told him. "It is to make sure this is the best place for you to be."

"Oh, okay then."

They were quiet talking amongst themselves the rest of the trip. The comments which reached Dani's ears were positive. This gave her hope.

She had called ahead to tell them she was coming back with the kids. Lizzy and Ella had Teddy and Amy busy in the kitchen creating something special for dinner and a special dessert.

When they arrived at the house, Dani led the children upstairs to the linen closet. They went in together.

"I understand Ella has a dinner surprise for all of you," Dani told them.

"Cool," Billy said, he'd already climbed on the lower bunk with his hand held video game.

Lucy crawled onto the daybed. She could hardly keep her eyes open. "Lucy," Grace said, "I don't want you falling asleep before dinner."

"Okay, Gracie," Lucy whispered as she picked up her blanket and baby doll.

Joey had headed to the bathroom.

Grace turned to Dani as she started to leave, "Miss Dani, thank you and Mr. Eli for everything. We can't stay here long, the kids need to be able to run and play, so if you can speed up this process, I'd be grateful."

"I'll do my best, Grace," Dani assured her, then she went back up the tunnel into the linen closet and headed to her office.

MAUREEN GREETED HER, "We had a couple of calls for wills and estate planning I put them on your schedule for mid-week. How did it go today?"

"The defense lawyer, some guy named Becker, tried to get Grace to admit she made the whole thing up. Grace was awesome."

"What about the couple the kids were going to meet?"

Dani thought a minute before answering, "The younger kids would move in tomorrow. Grace believes it is the right thing to do for the younger ones. They had a grand time, but I still have reservations. I can't keep them where they are indefinitely. They need time to run and play like they did today. This weekend they will be with the Nichols. It will be good for them."

She walked into her office and sat at her desk, a cup of coffee materialized next to her. She looked up to see Maureen had poured it and Teddy and Amy had arrived with a sandwich and some cookies.

"Thanks, guys, I needed this," she told them.

"We knew you were busy this morning," Teddy told her.

"And you forget to eat lunch, Miss Dani," Amy scolded her.

"What am I going to do when your new home is ready?" she chuckled.

"Miss us," Amy declared.

"Yes, I will miss you." She ruffled Amy's hair as she led them to her door. "I still have to work, but I will eat. Thank you."

"She means get lost," Teddy said taking Amy's hand and leaving the office.

Dani smiled, went back to her desk, picked up half the sandwich, and took a big bite. She was hungry. Eli was going to talk to the Nichols and when she heard from them she would know better how to feel about the situation. *For now it was her job to keep them safe until final arguments tomorrow. The weekend would be good for them, she knew in her heart. She hoped she would never have to care for children under these circumstances again. Keeping children cooped inside all day was wrong on all levels. Seemed more like prison than rescue.* Shaking her head, Dani picked up her dishes and took them to the kitchen. Then she returned to her office. She did have work to do.

CHAPTER FOURTEEN

The jury returned a verdict of guilty for James Dutton. Dani went from there to another courtroom where, Mr. Becker would again represent James Dutton in a custody hearing over his children.

Judge McAdams was already seated. "Bailiff, call the next case."

"Montgomery vs Dutton on the custody of the Dutton children."

Dani rose as her name was read and stepped to the table on the right. Becker came blustering through the door and took the defendant's table on the left.

"Are we ready to proceed?" the judge asked.

"Yes, your Honor," Dani replied.

"Yes, your Honor," Becker affirmed.

"Miss Montgomery, proceed."

"Your Honor, Mr. Dutton has been found guilty of child molestation of his eldest daughter. As the children's guardian, I would like to move the court severe all parental rights of James Dutton for Grace Dutton, Joseph Dutton, William Dutton, and Lucy Dutton."

"Objection!" Becker bellowed coming to his feet.

"What are your grounds for objection, Mr. Becker?" the judge asked.

"Mr. Dutton provides a home for the children. How can he do so if the children are taken away from him?"

"Your objection is overruled. It is out of order," Judge McAdams replied. "Is there anything you'd like to add Miss Montgomery?"

"Yes, your Honor," Dani responded, "a couple has come forward and are prepared to adopt all four children so they will not have to be separated. We'd like the Dutton family home sold to help with this transition."

Becker knocked over his chair getting to his feet, "This is preposterous! What is the man going to do for a home when he gets out of prison?"

"Mr. Becker, what your client does for housing in fifteen to thirty years is not the concern of this court," the judge informed him. "The placement of these children in a loving home is. I'm severing all parental rights from Mr. Dutton as the home he has provided for the past seven and half years has not been safe. The sale of this home is to be commenced immediately. Allow the children to remove any and all mementos they'd like, then sell the house forthwith." His gavel came down before Becker could even get a word out. "Ten minute recess."

"All rise," the bailiff said as the judge rose and left the room.

Dani felt she had crossed a big hurdle. The children would return to the house one more time and then all the items left would be sold or given away and the house would be sold. Money could be put in trust for their college educations. It was a good day.

"Don't think for a moment you've won," Becker sneered at her.

"I have," Dani countered.

"I'm going to appeal," Becker snapped.

"You are wasting your time," Dani told him. "The judge was within her rights to order as she did."

Becker was beyond her and turned to say, "We'll just see about that."

Dani watched him push and shove his way out of the court-room. She'd worry about him another day. It was time to give the children the good news. She would make arrangements to have Macy accompany them when they went for the last time.

She left the courthouse heading for her car and the ride home. On the way, she called Maureen to tell her she was coming.

"Well, it's been quiet here," Maureen told her.

"Good I need some quiet," Dani assured her. *Her mind drifted to Brad. She had not seen him since they rescued the children two weeks ago. She was missing him.*

Grabbing her cell she dialed his number. "Brad Stevens."

"Hey there good looking, where are you," she asked.

"Half way between Rivers Edge and Willow Bend," he answered, "Where are you?"

"Leaving Rivers Edge, shall I pick up some lunch?"

"Nope, I'm going to give you an address so pull off the road and punch it into your GPS."

Dani pulled off the side of the road put Brad on speaker and listened as he gave her the address. She put in it her GPS and told him she was on her way.

"I can't wait," he told her.

"Me, either." Hanging up she got back on the road and followed the directions. It took her less than ten minutes to find the work site Brad was overseeing.

"Hey, there beautiful," he said as she got out of her car. "How did court go this morning?"

"Is there somewhere we can get lunch?" she asked as he pulled her into his arms for a kiss.

"Sure, can we take your car?"

"Yes," was her breathless reply. Turning to go back to her car, Brad followed. Once inside he gave her directions.

They found the little out of the way Mexican restaurant Eli had told him about when they were scouting properties for Lizzy and her kids. He and Dani found a booth away from other customers. The waitress came and took their orders returning quickly with their drinks.

"Okay, tell me about your morning," Brad said after taking a swig of his beer.

"Mr. Dutton will serve fifteen to thirty years for molesting Grace and beating his sons. In family court they severed his parental rights and will be putting his house up for sale to help the children transition to a new life. The children will be able to go through the house one more time to get anything they still want. Then a sale will be held to get rid of furniture any not sold will be donated to Habitat for Humanity. A cleaning crew will come in and thoroughly clean the house. A team will go through and put a fresh coat of paint on the walls and the outside will be spruced up, then the house will be sold. Any taxes will be paid and the rest of the money will go into a trust for the children. If they end up with the Nichols, I will transfer the trust to them," she told him before taking a drink of her margarita.

"Wow, you've been busy."

She laughed, "I guess I have. I just want the children to have a good home."

"Sounds like you have a start," Brad told her.

"Speaking of starts, the children will be gone all weekend," Dani gave him her best seductive look.

"Dinner Saturday night, my house and church, Sunday morning," Brad suggested.

"Sounds like a plan."

Lunch came and they settled into eating. After lunch they headed back to the worksite. Brad reached over and held Dani's hand.

"Have I told you lately, how proud I am of the work you do?"

"A girl always likes compliments," she responded.

He leaned across the seat to pull her into his arms and give her a kiss, "I'll see you on Saturday." He got out of the car and headed back to work.

Dani drove home to see what other work she could get done before she went to tell the children the news.

CHAPTER FIFTEEN

In the hidden room the children had made a thank you card for Cara and Bryce. Then they found a game to play together. Grace set the boys at the laptops after lunch and put Lucy down for a nap. The boys worked on their school assignments and Grace pulled out a book to read. They heard Dani making her way down to them.

Quietly, Dani sat at the table and motioned for Grace to join them. Joey and Billy closed the laptops to hear what she had to say.

"First, your father has been sentenced to fifteen to thirty years. If he behaves, he will be out after fifteen years," Dani told them. "In family court, the judge decided he was no longer fit to be your father and severed his rights. She also is making the house available for you to go through one more time and choose any items you want to take with you into your new home. Anything you don't want, will be sold or donated. Then a cleaning crew will come in and thoroughly clean. A painting crew will paint every room and a gardener will spruce the front and back yards. We will put the house up for sale. The money from the sale will go into a trust fund for you. I will manage the fund until your adoption into a new family and then your parents will manage it."

Grace spoke first, "Can we schedule the last visit for the weekend? Then anything we want to take could go right to Cara and Bryce's."

"I'll see what I can do."

"Does this mean we divorced our dad?" Joey asked.

"It's almost like a divorce," Dani told him. "It means your dad is no longer your dad."

"Good," Billy said. "I didn't like him."

"And he can't come get us in fifteen years?" Joey persisted.

"Once you are adopted, he can't come get you ever," Dani assured him. "You can even change your name to your adoptive parents' name."

"Billy Nichols, I like it."

Grace reached across the table to ruffle his hair with her hand, "Silly, you'd like any name you could choose."

"Yep, but I like Bryce and I'd like to be his son."

Dani smiled, "Then we'll see if we can make it happen."

Grace gave her a shy smile and said, "Thank you."

"It is my pleasure," Dani said. "Now I still have work to do and Ella will be bringing dinner soon." She stood and made her way out of the chamber feeling this would be a good thing for the kids.

Friday night came sooner than anyone anticipated. The kids were ready to go and on the front porch when Cara and Bryce arrived. They were going to take the kids to dinner then home. Tomorrow bright and early they would take the kids to go through their old home, have some lunch, and head back to the ranch. The kids would be back by dinner time on Sunday.

Dani felt sad and happy as she watched them leave. Sad the children went through this and happy Eli had found someone to take them all. She did not want them going into the foster care system where they would most likely have been separated. She went inside to close her office and get ready for dinner with Lizzy and her kids. *They, too will soon be leaving, Dani told herself. Time to dig into the Chelsie Patton file again and see if she could find closure for those families.*

Six weeks later

Dani said her last good-byes to the Dutton children. She would represent them during the adoption in a few weeks. They made a wonderful family. The Nichols already enrolled them in school, they would start on Monday. The on-line courses showed they were able to handle even those types of classes. She was happy to see Grace responding to both Cara and Bryce. Lucy and the boys were already calling them Mom and Dad. They still had months to the final adoption, but the judge allowed for a name change and all four children were known as the Nichols kids. It made Dani smile. She provided sanctuary while making it possible for these children to escape the life they were living and create a new more positive one.

Brad came to join her on the porch, "Are you ready for dinner?"

Turning with a smile on her face she responded, "I am."

Holding hands they walked into the house and headed toward the dining room to join Lizzy, Teddy, and Amy for dinner.

SPECIAL PREVIEW OF THE UPCOMING
MACY McVANNEL MYSTERY

SOMETHING BORROWED, SOMETHING BLUE

COMING 2015

SOMETHING BORROWED, SOMETHING BLUE

CHAPTER ONE

Being jolted awake on a Saturday morning could not be good. I looked at the clock. It read seven-thirty. "McVannel."

"I said yes!" screamed the excited female voice on the other end.

Shaking myself awake I asked, "Dani? Do you have any idea what time it is?"

"Of course," she laughed. "I let you sleep until eight-thirty."

Rolling over I looked at the clock again, she was right. "What is so all fired important on a Saturday morning?"

"Macy, pay attention. Brad asked me to marry him and I said yes."

I sat straight up in the bed. "What? When? Details," I demanded.

"Well, when you drag yourself out of bed, you can meet me at Le Café. I'll treat," Dani told me.

Throwing my feet over the side of the bed I headed for the bathroom. "Give me thirty minutes."

"You got it."

I heard Dani giggle as she hung up the phone. Hopping into the shower I thought, *This time she has lost her mind. We can hash it all out as soon as I get to the restaurant.*

I PULLED INTO the restaurant in less than thirty minutes. Dani was sitting in a booth midway back on the left. I walked toward her. Watching as her smile lit her entire face.

She stood and gave me hug. Hugging her back I extracted myself and sat down. Dani had ordered tea for me and cinnamon rolls.

"I told them to give us about five minutes and we'd order the rest of breakfast," she said.

"Okay spill it," I told her. "Just what happened and when?"

"After I left you yesterday, I got Margo Hunter to her pick up point. Then I drove home to get Misty Evons ready to leave. Brad and I took her down river and drove her to her pick up point. Once we dropped her off, Brad and I went to his place for dinner," Dani took a breath before continuing. "After dinner, Brad had me sit on the sofa. Then he brought me a bouquet of red roses, I put them to my nose to smell them and realized Brad was on his knees. I put the roses down and he asked me to be his wife. He had already asked Sam and Ella if it would be okay." She held out her hand so I could see her ring. It was a delicate piece of jewelry and looked like it had been made with Dani in mind.

"And you said yes, just like that? You didn't think of the hurt from the past? You said, yes?" I was amazed.

"Nothing from the past matters," Dani assured me. "He loves me, I love him. We want to spend our lives together. I said, yes without even thinking about it."

"Well, have you picked a date?"

"Not yet, but I want you to be my maid of honor."

"Me, you must be joking?"

Dani rolled her eyes, "Yes, you and no, I'm not joking."

Smiling I said, "I'm in."

The waitress came to take our order, Dani must have been starving she ordered bacon and an omelet. I settled for just crispy bacon.

"How are you going to fit a wedding in with all your projects?" I wanted to know.

"I'll find a way. I know it won't be until spring so we have some time," she told me.

"Any idea on color?"

"Something really different," she confessed as if she had something in mind.

"Please tell me you are not thinking some foolish retro tie-dye stuff."

Giggling she said, "Not a chance."

I breathed a sigh of relief and bit into my cinnamon roll. Dani just took a sip of coffee. I could see a dreamy look in her eye.

After breakfast we parted ways. I was not sure where Dani was off to, but I was hoping to catch an hour nap.

AT HOME I decided I might as well stay up. Eli and I had plans later. I headed upstairs, did the workout I missed this morning. Then I sorted the laundry and got started on it.

While I worked my mind wandered. *The first case Tom and I had really worked was the Appleton cold case. Out of it I had gained a family of sorts, Ida Appleton, Sally Mae Davis, JJ Waxman, Shannon and the kids, Mike West's mom Martha, and JJ's mom, Angela. It also brought Eli Patterson into my life.*

This last case had almost done me in. Chelsie Patton was evil like I have never encountered before and never want to again. Now I have to wonder if I have been wrong about this child all along. Is Dani right, did something happen to her when she was nine? Does it make all the things she has done okay?

Aside from the case, JJ and Sally Mae are having a June wedding. Eli and I have been asked to stand up with them. Now Dani drops on me, she and Brad are getting married and I'm to be the maid of honor. Wow, too much to handle. And what is going on with Eli and me? Is this where we are heading?

I was startled by the ringing of my phone. Didn't anyone know it was Saturday? "McVannel."

It's Tom, we have a case."

"Today? You've got to be kidding."

"Nope, I'm on my way to pick you up."

"I'll be ready. Hey, will I be home in time for dinner?"

"Don't count on it," he said hanging up.

Great as it I wanted a case today. I dialed Eli to tell him the news.

"Patterson."

"Hey, it's me. Tom called and we've got a case."

"Yeah, it's the same one I got. I'll see you in a bit."

I headed upstairs to change so I would look like a professional when we got to where we were going. This was not how my Saturdays were supposed to go.

ABOUT THE AUTHOR

Retired teacher Rebecka Vigus spends her time writing, reading, crocheting, hiking, and swimming. She travels seeking the ideal place to call home.

Crossing the Line is the second book in her Macy McVannel series. Book one *Cold Case: Sleeping Dogs Lie* was released in February, 2012. She is currently working on book three in the series.

Ms. Vigus has been writing since she was in her pre-teens. Her first book was poetry, *Only a Start and Beyond*. She also wrote a self-help book for tweens and teens; *So You Think You Want to be a Mommy?* She followed it with three mystery novels, *Secrets; Out of the Flames,* and *Target of Vengeance*. Ms. Vigus has been listed as a Michigan Author and Illustrator at the state of Michigan website.

She loves spending time with family and friends. She is the mother of one and grandmother of four. She finds time to crochet preemie layettes for a neo-natal unit as well as hiking and swimming.

Find her at *www.ramblingsbyrebecka.blogspot.com*. All of her books are available at *amazon.com* and *barnesandnoble.com*

www.ingramcontent.com/pod-product-compliance
Lightning Source LLC
Chambersburg PA
CBHW020316150626
46552CB00022B/2897